WHERE'S RODNEY?

by

CARMEN BOGAN

Illustrated by

FLOYD COOPER

Yosemite Conservancy
YOSEMITE NATIONAL PARK

"Rodney!
Where is Rodney?"

Once again Rodney wasn't in his seat,
and Miss Garcia had had enough.
But Rodney had interesting things to do.

Like watch a big black bird soar over the cafeteria that smelled like yesterday's lunch. Or catch a tiny pill bug creeping across the windowsill. He stood on his tippy toes to find the stray dog that bullied the neighborhood. Rodney was inside, but he wanted to be outside. Outside was where Rodney always wanted to be.

Miss Garcia let out a long, deep breath. She stepped behind Rodney and tapped him on the shoulder.

"Rodney, join the class. The word of the week is *majestic*," Miss Garcia said. "Ma-jes-tic. Can you tell us what it means?"

Rodney looked around the classroom. There were a million eyes looking back.

"Nope."

Miss Garcia took another deep breath.
Rodney balanced on one foot like a pink
flamingo. Sue Lin giggled and covered her mouth.
Then he hopped into the air like a cricket.
Coty chuckled. Then Rodney stretched out his
arms like an eagle soaring high above the...

"Sit down, Rodney!"

Miss Garcia said. The whole class
roared with laughter.

"Okay. *Majestic* means grand and beautiful. Rodney, if you can't do your work you won't be able to go on the field trip to the park on Friday."

But Rodney didn't care. He knew all about the park.
It was a small, triangle-shaped patch of yellow grass
next to the corner store and the bus stop. It had one
large cardboard trash can and two benches where
some grownups sat all day long.

Yes, Rodney knew the park well.
Anyway, Momma said to stay far
away from that park!

When the three o'clock bell rang, Rodney ran outside. He darted across the street past Miss Jackson, the crossing guard.

"Walk!" she yelled. But he ran. He ran past the corner store. He ran past the bus stop. Then he ran past the triangle-shaped patch of yellow grass and the two benches and the broken gate where the bully-dog slept.

Now he could see Momma peeping out the window.
She opened the door and gave him a big hug.

"I'm glad you're inside," she said. But outside
was where Rodney wanted to be.

Very early on Friday, the old yellow bus squeaked, jerked, and rattled out of the school parking lot. Even before it reached the front gate, Sue Lin and Amina were singing and playing clapping games. Everyone was excited. But not Rodney. And he knew that when they got to the park, they would all see that he was right. Parks are no big deal!

The bus turned the corner onto Second Street, but Rodney thought that the bus driver must be lost because he drove past the bus stop, past the corner store, and even past the patch of yellow grass. Sue Lin and Amina kept singing and clapping. The old school bus rumbled, rolled, and creaked farther and longer than Rodney had ever been.

Rodney gazed out the window. He stared at the white lines in the middle of the great highway. He counted the big trucks that passed the bus. He leaned to see the birds float above the fields of tall, dry grass. He watched the people in wide straw hats picking fruits and vegetables in neat rows.

The old bus clanked, coughed, and choked. It climbed higher and higher until a great mountain swallowed it whole. At the other end of the tunnel, the mountain spit out the old bus into a flash of sunshine. No one laughed, no one talked, and no one wiggled. Sue Lin and Amina even stopped singing.

"Look, everyone!" Miss Garcia announced. "It's the park!"

And finally,
Rodney was outside.

At the park, he was higher.

He was lower.

He was bigger.

He was smaller.

He was
louder.

He was
quieter.

He was faster.

He was slower.

Rodney was outside—
more outside than he
had ever been before.

The sun sank in the sky. It was time to leave. Some of the children chattered and giggled. Some munched on leftovers. Others dozed. Sue Lin and Amina sang more songs.

"Where's Rodney?" Miss Garcia asked. Rodney was sitting quietly, gazing out the window. Miss Garcia sat beside him. "Do you like the park, Rodney?"

"Oh, yes," he said softly.
"It's majestic!"

HOW TO VISIT A PARK

To have your own majestic experience in a park, start by researching county, state, or national parks. Many parks are accessible via public transportation; some will require having a car. Fees to enter parks will vary. Check to see if the park is offering a fee-free day. Be sure to bring a backpack containing water for the day (at least one liter), snacks, and lunch for a picnic. Also bring sun protection, extra clothing, and athletic or hiking shoes. It is a good idea to have a map of where you are going, which can be found at most park visitor centers; a cell phone or GPS may not always work.

For a more structured experience in nature, consider a program sponsored by a park partner. Park partners are organizations whose purpose is to support parks and the enjoyment of them. You can join an expert naturalist guide for a walk or trek, or arrange for a group visit to your favorite park. Yosemite Conservancy provides Custom Outdoor Adventure programs to help families connect with the wonders of Yosemite National Park. NatureBridge offers schools, students, and families multi-day environmental education programs in six national park locations. You can find similar organizations at many parks.

However you plan to visit a park, the most important thing is to have fun in a special, protected place that belongs to *all* people. It can be a life-changing experience!

ABOUT DREAM ON PUBLISHING

Dream On Publishing is an independent multicultural children's book publisher established in 2013 by author Carmen Bogan. Our goal is to promote literacy for children of color by producing high-quality children's literature that reflects their interests and their lives. We believe that every child deserves to read about characters that look like them, celebrate their cultures, and lift up their legacies. Dream On Publishing is proud to partner with Yosemite Conservancy on this book.

Yosemite Conservancy inspires people to support projects and programs that preserve Yosemite and enrich the visitor experience.

YOSEMITE CONSERVANCY.
yosemiteconservancy.org

naturebridge.org

For Willie, Erin, and Natalie –C.B.

For Niko –F.C.

Text copyright © 2017 by Carmen M. Bogan
Illustrations copyright © 2017 by Floyd Cooper

Published in the United States by Yosemite Conservancy.

Library of Congress Control Number: 2016961525

Design by Katie Jennings Campbell

ISBN 978-1-930238-73-2
Printed in China by Toppan Leefung, February 2017

1 2 3 4 5 6 – 21 20 19 18 17